topps® LEAGUE Story

UP!

· BOOK SIX ·

By **Kurtis Scaletta**

Illustrated by **Ethen Beavers**

Amulet Books
New York

For Byron, keeping his streak
alive as the best kid in the world
—K.S.

For Mom
—E.B.

Cataloging-in-Publication Data has been applied for and
may be obtained from the Library of Congress.

ISBN 978-1-4197-0727-8 (paperback)

Book design by Chad W. Beckerman

Published in 2013 by Amulet Books, an imprint of
ABRAMS. All rights reserved. No portion of this book may
be reproduced, stored in a retrieval system, or transmitted
in any form or by any means, mechanical, electronic,
photocopying, recording, or otherwise, without written
permission from the publisher. Amulet Books and Amulet
Paperbacks are registered trademarks of Harry N.
Abrams, Inc.

Printed and bound in U.S.A.
10 9 8 7 6 5 4 3 2 1

Amulet Books are available at special discounts when
purchased in quantity for premiums and promotions as
well as fundraising or educational use. Special editions
can also be created to specification. For details, contact
specialsales@abramsbooks.com or the address below.

ABRAMS
THE ART OF BOOKS SINCE 1949

115 West 18th Street
New York, NY 10011
www.abramsbooks.com

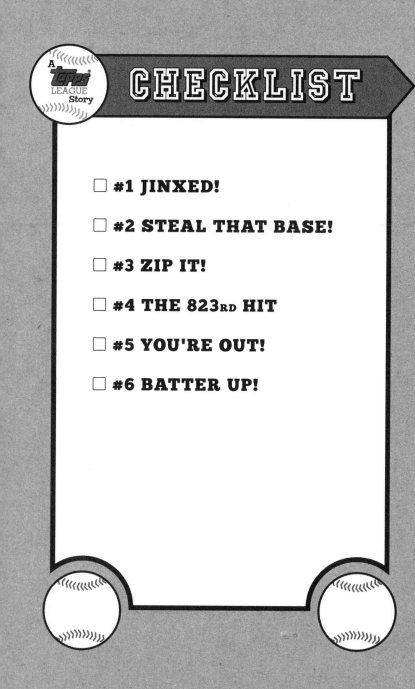

A topps LEAGUE Story

CHECKLIST

I woke up an hour earlier than I had to, thanks to the sound of whistling from the kitchen. Dad is a morning person and a whistler. I tried to ignore it, but I also smelled bacon and pancakes. That was too good to ignore, so I got dressed and headed downstairs.

Dad was at the stove, poking at the bacon. He was still whistling. Our dog, Penny, was perched right by him, staring hungrily and whimpering. She carried a better tune than he did.

"Grmdg," I said. It was the best I could do.

"Good morning to you too!"

He handed me a plate of food, and I sat down to eat. I felt a lot more awake after a few bites.

"Thanks, but what happened to Mom?" Usually she made breakfast on Sundays.

"She's playing golf with friends," he said. "They wanted to hit the links before it started raining. Speaking of which, maybe you won't have to work today. Sounds like it's going to come down pretty hard later."

"I sure hope not." I was a batboy for the Pine City Porcupines, the Single-A team in our hometown. It was really fun, and way better than sitting around on a rainy day.

• • •

Dad was right. The sky was dark and gloomy, and looked like it might let loose any second with a storm. But they don't cancel baseball games unless they absolutely have to. I walked to the ballpark and got ready for the day's game against the Centralville Cougars. I made coffee, set up the bat rack, and made sure the supply chest was full.

The players started coming in.

"I bet we don't play today," said Wayne Zane. He was the Porcupines' catcher.

"Hope I can get some bull-pen time in," said Ryan Kimball, the closer. A closer is a pitcher who only plays late in the game, when the team is protecting a small lead.

Diego Prado said something in Spanish. Diego was a bench player. That meant he mostly sat in the dugout and waited. Sometimes he would get a turn at the plate or an inning in the outfield.

"He says he hopes to play every day," Lance Pantaño translated. Lance was a pitcher from

Puerto Rico and was fluent in both Spanish and English. Diego was from Mexico and spoke only Spanish.

I knew how Diego felt. That's what it was like for me when I played Little League. I got to play, but never for the whole game.

"You'll get a chance. Just be patient," said Sammy Solaris, the designated hitter. "You're good in the outfield, and you've been hitting well in batting practice."

Lance started to translate, but Diego waved at him to stop. *"Entiendo,"* he said, which must have meant, "I understand."

• • •

It was drizzling when the game started. The umpires met and decided the game could be played. It wasn't raining very hard, at least not yet. The fans wore ponchos or raincoats. Some made their programs into hats.

In the top of the second inning, a Cougar batter hit a fly ball to deep left field. Danny O'Brien ran after it, skidded on the damp grass, lost his balance, and fell down. The ball bounced all the way to the wall. Danny tried to get up, but he was clearly hurt. Myung Young ran from center field to get the ball. The batter ran all the way to third base.

After the play, the trainer helped Danny off the field.

"Are you all right?" I asked Danny as he passed through the dugout. He looked like he was in a lot of pain.

"I just twisted my ankle," he said. "I'll be OK."

"Prado, you're in," said Grumps, the manager of the Porcupines. His full name was Harry Humboldt, but everyone called him Grumps. He made the change on his scorecard.

"Gracias," said Diego. He got his glove and ran out to play left field.

He got a base hit in his first turn at the plate, and batted in a run.

The rain started coming down a lot harder in the sixth inning. The game was called, but enough innings had been played for the game to be official.

Danny O'Brien was still in the locker room after the game. He had his leg stretched out on the bench, and ice packs were taped to his ankle. He was reading a paperback book.

"How are you doing, Danny?" Wayne Zane asked him.

"I'm good," said Danny. He closed the book, using his finger to mark his place.

"Are you sure?" asked Tommy, the third baseman. "It looked like a bad spill."

"Sure I'm sure," said Danny with a wince.

"It doesn't even hurt that much. Really." He opened his book again, but he didn't look happy.

I sat on the bench to towel off some of the equipment. I liked hanging around the players after the game, when they were joking around and ribbing each other.

"Hey, what are you reading?" Wayne asked Danny.

"Trouble on the Mound," said Danny. "It's a Mike McKay mystery."

"Oh, yeah. Mike McKay, the Sports Detective! I've read all of them," said Wayne. "I think that's the one where the pitching coach put the poison in the rosin bag."

"Hey!" Danny said, sputtering. "I'm only on page thirty—you just spoiled the ending!"

"Oops." Wayne went to his locker. Danny chucked the book, and it bounced off the locker door next to Wayne.

"You missed," said Wayne. "Good thing you're not a pitcher."

I was right there, so I picked up the book and handed it back to Danny.

"Do I get three throws for a dollar?" he asked me.

I laughed. "Sure."

"I'll get you the dollar," joked Teddy Larrabee, the first baseman.

Diego Prado walked by on his way to his locker.

"Nice hit, today," Danny told him, offering a hand. Diego slapped it.

"Gracias."

"I might need a few days to heal," said Danny. "Hope you're ready to play every day."

Diego answered in Spanish.

"He hopes he is, and he's sorry you're hurt," said Lance.

"Tell him 'Thanks,' and I'll be fine," said Danny to Lance.

"He knows," said Lance. "He understands almost everything you guys say. He just can't *speak* English."

Diego nodded and said something else in Spanish.

"He says he knows enough English to get Wayne's jokes," said Lance.

"Poor guy," said Danny.

• • •

Dylan returned from the other dugout. He was the other batboy, and he had been in the visitors' dugout helping the Cougars.

"Hey, Wally," he said to the clubhouse manager, who was our boss. "I have something important to talk to you about."

"What's up?"

"It's kind of . . . secret," said Dylan, looking around the locker room.

"OK. Let's meet in my office." Wally's office was nothing but a desk in the equipment room, but Dylan followed him in there.

I was dressed and ready to leave. Then I remembered that it was still raining, so I looked for my rainproof poncho. Wally had given both Dylan and me Porcupine ponchos a while back.

My locker was kind of a mess. I had extra clothes, game-day souvenirs, and a bunch of

other junk. I kept meaning to sort it out but never got around to it.

Dylan came back and grabbed his poncho from his locker.

"What's going on?" I asked.

"I'm going to miss most of the next home stand the week after next."

"Really?" The next home stand was going to be the longest of the season, with games on ten straight days. "How come?"

"I've got other plans." He closed his locker door. "Wally's going to try and find a replacement."

"OK." I expected Dylan to tell me why he would be gone, but he didn't.

"Are you ready to walk home?" he asked.

"Sure." I finally found my poncho hiding in the corner of my locker, under a baseball glove I used during batting practice.

We headed out. We walked with our hoods up and our heads lowered because it was raining really hard. Dylan had plenty of time to tell me where he was going, but he didn't say a word. I wondered what the big secret was and why he wouldn't tell me.

Monday was a day off, so Dylan and I went for a bike ride. It had stopped raining and the sun was out. We stopped at the golf course clubhouse to have a Coke and cool off. You don't have to play golf to use the clubhouse.

"How's Penny?" Dylan asked. He had taken care of her when my family was on vacation. He was crazy about animals.

"She's fine," I told him. Penny did mope around for two days because she missed Dylan, but she was getting better. "Hey, do you need somebody to take care of your rabbits while you're gone?"

"No. My parents can take care of them," he said.

So his parents weren't going with him. That was a clue! Was Dylan going to camp? Was he visiting relatives on his own? And why would either of those things be a secret? Why couldn't he just tell me?

I needed Mike McKay, the Sports Detective, to help me crack the case. That gave me an idea.

"Want to stop at the library on the way home?"

"Yeah, sure."

We finished our Cokes and went to get our bikes, which were locked up by the putting green. Dylan nudged me.

"Look who's practicing."

I glanced over and saw a guy in bright checkered pants.

"Ernie Hecker!" I whispered. Ernie was the biggest loudmouth in all of Pine City. He came to every Porcupines game and sat behind the visitors' dugout so he could yell at the opposing players.

He glanced over at us. "Boys, it's rude to talk when a player is getting ready to take a swing," he said. "Even if it's just a practice shot."

He must not have recognized us without our batboy uniforms.

"Sorry," said Dylan.

"Me too," I said. I knew that Ernie was right, but he was the last person on earth who should complain about other people talking!

"Shh!" Ernie lined up the putt, took his swing, and missed the hole by a foot. "Darn it!

I would have made that if you hadn't distracted me." He glared at us both.

It was all we could do to get to our bikes and pedal away before we burst out laughing.

• • •

We pedaled over to the library. Dylan got three different books about horses. I got four paperback mysteries about Mike McKay, the Sports Detective.

"You're going to read grown-up books?" Dylan asked me.

"I'm getting them for Danny," I told him. "If he has to rest his ankle, he'll want something to do."

We went to the self-check-out table. I slid one of the books across the scanner, and a card fell out.

"Hey!" said Dylan. "It's a baseball card."

Sure enough, it was a real baseball card. It

looked old, and part of the front was peeled off. Across the top was the name Ozzie Virgil. I had a card for a player named Ozzie Virgil Jr., but it was from the 1980s. This must have been his dad!

"The last person to check out that book must have used it as a bookmark and forgotten about it," said Dylan.

"I wonder if there's any way to get the card back to him?"

"Or her," Dylan added.

"Right."

Who said a woman couldn't collect baseball cards and read sports mysteries?

We went to the reference desk. The librarian was clacking away on a computer.

"Excuse me, can we look up the last person who had this book?" I asked. "He or she left something in it."

"Sorry," he said. "I can look up who has a book checked out now, but not everyone who ever checked it out. What did you find?"

"An old baseball card."

"Hmm." He took the book and scanned it. "It hasn't been checked out for weeks. If the borrower was going to call about the card, he or she would have done so by now. I guess it's your lucky day."

"Thanks." The card probably wasn't worth a bazillion dollars, but I felt a little weird keeping it.

"Maybe you can give it to one of the Porcupines to help them out of a jam," said Dylan. "You've done that so many times before, I've lost count."

"Maybe." Some of the Porcupines thought my baseball cards were magic. I thought the cards just reminded them of what was possible.

The player on the card had always done something amazing.

Had Ozzie Virgil done anything that was extraordinary?

• • •

I looked him up on the Internet when I got home. I read that Ozzie bounced between the minor leagues and the big leagues, mostly as a utility player. His claim to fame was that he was the first person from the Dominican Republic to play in the big leagues.

Virgil was probably a nice guy, but if the card had any magic in it, I didn't know what it was. I decided to leave the card in the library book for now. It seemed like that was where it belonged.

For the first time, I really looked at the cover of the book. The title was *Never Get Back*. I flipped it over and started reading the summary.

When a minor league batboy named Charlie goes missing . . .

It was about a minor league batboy? And his name was *Charlie*? This kid and I had the same job—and the same name! "Charlie" and "Chad" were both nicknames for Charles. It was kind of cool but also kind of spooky. I needed to know whether the batboy in this book ended up alive and well.

I opened it up and started reading.

Charlie worked for a team called the Cactus City Scorpions. One day he disappeared right in the middle of a game. Mike McKay, the Sports Detective,

was called in to figure out what happened to him. It turned out that Charlie had a really big baseball card collection. Mike McKay suspected that one of the rare and valuable cards might be missing. That part made my heart beat faster. The Charlie character was *way* too much like me. I put the book down, afraid to read any further.

I would have peeked at the ending, but I didn't want to spoil it for myself. I was no Wayne Zane.

3

was halfway to work the next day when I remembered I'd forgotten to bring Danny's books! I ran home, barged in the front door, and bounded up the stairs to my room.

The books were all there, with a sticky note on the top one that said, "Remember to give to Danny!" The note hadn't done any good because I had forgotten to read it.

I grabbed the stack and ran back down the stairs.

"What's going on?" Mom asked.

"Nothing," I said, wheezing. "Everything is fine." I hurried out the door and headed for the ballpark.

I'd just stowed the books in my locker and started getting dressed when Danny hobbled into the locker room wearing a plastic boot. He looked miserable.

"I'm not going to be able to play for at least two weeks," he announced. "I have a sprained ankle. I can't put any weight on my foot."

"Oh, man. That's rough." Sammy patted him on the shoulder.

"We've all been there once or twice," said Wayne. "Hang in there."

"Thanks, guys," said Danny. "This is hard. I really want to play."

"Hope these will help pass the time," I said. I gave him three books about Mike McKay, the Sports Detective. I'd decided to keep the one about the missing batboy, even if I was scared to read it.

"Hey, thanks! That's really thoughtful of you." Danny flipped through the books. "I think I'll read this one first. *Point Blank After Touchdown.*"

Wayne opened his mouth.

"Shut up, Wayne," Danny told him before he could get a word out. "I want to find out how it ends by *reading* it."

"I was just going to say it's a good one," said Wayne. But you could tell he was itching to blurt out the ending. "One of my favorites. Never would have guessed that . . ."

Before he could get another word out, Sammy clapped a hand over his mouth. "Do you promise not to spoil his book?"

Wayne nodded, and Sammy let go.

Diego picked up one of the other two books. He muttered something in Spanish.

"Good idea," said Lance.

"Huh?" asked Sammy.

"He said reading the book might improve his English," said Lance.

"So would *speaking* English," said Wayne. "Just sayin'."

"He's right," said Lance. "Don't be afraid of making mistakes," he told Diego. "The only way you can get better is by trying."

Diego answered in Spanish.

Lance translated for the rest of us. "He'll work on baseball for now and on speaking English later. He has a big hole to fill in left field."

• • •

Diego got three base hits that day, and the Porcupines won the game.

"Way to go, Diego," Danny told him after the game. "You've been playing really well."

"*Gracias,*" said Diego.

"Keep it up, buddy," said Wayne. He clapped Diego on the back. Then he saw that Danny was a third of the way into *Point Blank After Touchdown.*

"You're a fast reader," he said. "Is the coach still alive?"

"What? Of course he is! Why wouldn't he be?"

"Um . . . that's why I asked," said Wayne. "Why wouldn't he be?"

"You rat," said Danny. "Why do you keep spoiling the ending?"

"I didn't!" Wayne said. "I only spoiled the middle."

"Well, keep it to yourself," said Danny. He flipped the page and resumed reading. "OK, they just found the coach under the bleachers."

"Told you," said Wayne.

"I know you told me. That's the problem."

"Sorry," said Wayne. "I'm just excited to talk about those books with someone."

I decided I would read my book as soon as I got home. I needed to know if Charlie ended up safe and sound.

• • •

"You must be worried about someone," Dylan told me as we crossed the parking lot.

"Me? Really? Why do you think that?"

"You're chewing on your lower lip and you just muttered 'I sure hope he's OK' under your breath."

"Oh." I felt silly. Charlie was a make-believe character. Dylan might not understand. "I was thinking about Danny," I lied. It was a very small lie, because I *was* worried about Danny's ankle and how fast it would heal.

"Yeah," he said. "I hope he gets better soon. Oh, by the way. You don't have to worry about me being gone."

"Really? You found a replacement?"

"Diego's brother Ricky is coming to visit. He really wants to be a batboy himself, and this will be a chance for him to learn the ropes."

"That's great," I agreed. "Perfect timing."

"We'll even have a few days for both of us to help him learn," said Dylan. "See you tomorrow!" We split off toward our own homes.

I thought about Charlie, the batboy in the book, and started running. I really wanted to know what happened to him, even if I was scared to find out.

4

The problem was, I couldn't find the book anywhere! I looked under my bed. I looked on the bedside table. I looked on the desk. I looked in the bathroom. I looked in the living room and in the kitchen. I even looked in the refrigerator. Maybe I got a glass of milk and accidentally put the book away instead of the milk?

I was desperate!

"Dad, did you find a mystery book and start reading it?" I asked.

He usually read factual books about topics

like tree moss and President Carter. Maybe he wanted to read a fun book for a change.

"You're reading a murder mystery?" he asked. One of his eyebrows went way up.

"No, it's just a missing-person mystery," I said. Who said anything about murder?

"Hmm. Well, it sounds like you have a missing-book mystery too," said Dad.

I groaned. Did Dad have to make a joke about this?

I kept searching, but pretty soon I ran out of places to look. I would never know what happened to Charlie! I would also have to pay for the book, but that didn't seem as important. I was really worried about that kid.

• • •

Diego got a base hit the next day, and two the day after that. That made four games in a row with at least one hit.

Then the Porcupines went on the road. They had three games against the Swedenberg Swatters and four more against the Heron Lake Humdingers. I didn't like it when the team went on long road trips. Dylan and I didn't travel with them, and I missed going to the ballpark. Plus, I got bored.

I listened to the Porcupines' games on the radio. The first night, Diego got two hits, and the Porcupines won. He got another hit in the next night's game, and *three* hits the day after that.

When a player goes several games in a row with a hit, they call it a "hitting streak." He doesn't have to get a hit every time he comes to the plate, just one per game. Diego officially had a streak going: seven games in a row.

Every day, he got another hit and added to the streak: eight games . . . nine games . . . then ten games. He probably wouldn't break any records, but it was fun and exciting to see the number going up.

The Porcupines played the last game of their road trip on Thursday afternoon. My friend Casey came over to listen with me. He brought his newest baseball cards so he could compare them with my baseball cards.

"I need six more cards to have all of the NL players," he told me. "I need three more for the AL."

"Look through my extras," I told him. I gave him the bundle, and he started sorting through them, commenting as he went.

"Got it . . . got it . . . got it. Ooh, I don't have this one." He set it aside. "Shh."

"I'm not talking."

"Shh!" he said again and waved his hand. "Prado is batting."

He was right. Diego came up to the plate, and the announcers reminded the listeners he had at least one hit in every game since he'd started playing full-time.

Neither of us breathed while Diego batted. He swung on the third pitch and scorched it into left field.

"Hooray!" I threw my hands in the air.

"Woo-hoo!" Casey threw his hands in the air too.

"Since when do you care?" I asked. Casey loved baseball, but he didn't root for the Porcupines. He was originally from Rosedale and was a fan of the Rogues.

"He has an eleven-game hitting streak going," he said. "It's cool. Besides, my uncle Marvin and I are going to all three games when the Rogues come to town. It'll be cool to see him add to his streak. I hope he does—as long as the Rogues still win."

"That *would* be cool," I said. "Except for the Rogues winning. But I heard their pitching's gone downhill."

"Our pitchers are all rookies," he admitted. "We used to have the best pitchers in the Prairie League, but they all got called up."

"That's what you get for being good," I said. "Is Damien Ricken at Double-A?"

"Triple-A!" he said. "He's doing great."

I was glad to hear it. Damien was a nice guy. The Rogues were the Porcupines' biggest rivals, but I could dislike the team and still like the individual players.

"I think the Porcupines should make Diego Prado their full-time left fielder," said Casey.

"The Porcupines already have a full-time left fielder," I reminded him. "His name is Danny O'Brien."

"Danny O'Brien," said Casey, followed by a *pftpftpft* noise.

"Come on," I said. "Danny's great."

"You say that about all the Porcupines," said Casey. "If you were the manager, would you bench Diego Prado in the middle of a hitting streak?"

"No," I admitted.

"Exactly," he said.

"Fine," I agreed. Diego's hitting streak was exciting, but I wondered what would happen when Danny O'Brien got healthy enough to play again.

5

The first three things I noticed on Friday were a boy I didn't know, the tub-sized sink by the laundry machines, and an armful of bats. I noticed them all at once, because the boy I didn't know was dropping an armload of bats into the sink, which was full of hot sudsy water.

"Ack!" I nudged the boy out of the way and rescued the bats from the sink. "What are you doing?!"

"Helping!" said the boy. He was about a year younger than me and had dark hair.

"Thanks for trying, but we don't clean bats that way," I told him.

"Why not?"

"We just don't." The bats would probably be OK getting wet once, but over time the wood would get soft and ruined. I leaned the bats against the wall to dry. "I'll show you the right way to clean them later," I told him. "Glad it was just a few bats."

"I did a lot more than that," he said, pointing at a canvas bag.

"You put them away wet?"

"I put them back where I found them," he said, beaming.

"Uh-oh." I took the bats out and lined them up along every available wall space to dry. The new kid helped.

"By the way, I'm Chad," I said, and offered my hand.

"I know! Diego told me about you." We shook hands. His was still wet and soapy. "He said you are the best batboy in the world. He said I would learn everything I needed to know from you. I'm Ricky, his little brother."

"I figured that out," I told him. "Thanks for helping. Where is Diego, anyway?"

"Practicing his batting."

"Already?" The other players wouldn't be going out for BP for a long time.

"He's been playing well and wants to keep it up. He told me to wait for you and not touch anything. Um, don't tell him I touched anything. *Please?*"

"I won't," I said.

"Thanks!"

"You speak English really well," I told him. "You don't even have an accent."

"Thanks! They teach English at my school,

and it's my best subject. Diego said I can be his personal translator while I'm here."

"Hey, guys," said Wayne. He was often the first player to arrive. "You having a meeting with the bats?"

"Yeah, I gave them a little pre-game pep speech," I said.

"Good one."

"By the way, this is Ricky," I told him. "He's Diego's brother. He's going to be a temporary batboy."

"Hey, Ricky. Your *little* brother is playing really great," said Wayne as he shook Ricky's hand.

"Diego is older than me by eleven years!" said Ricky.

"I was just kidding you," said Wayne.

Ricky laughed. "You must be Wayne, the really funny catcher?"

"That's me. Diego said I was really funny?" Wayne puffed out his chest a bit. "You know, when I'm done with baseball I want to be a comedian."

"You'll be great," said Ricky.

"I like this kid," said Wayne. "He can be a batboy for me anytime."

"Hey, everyone!" Lance Pantaño came in. "Ready to take on the Rogues?"

"Hey, Lance. You have to meet this new batboy," said Wayne. "He's got great taste in comedy."

"I need my coffee first." Lance got his mug from his locker. It was a Porcupines mug with masking tape plastered on it and "Property of Lance" written on it.

"Oh, I forgot to make coffee!" I realized.

"It's fine. I made it," said Ricky.

"You did?" I asked.

"I made it extra good, with lots of milk and sugar," he said.

I suddenly realized there was a burning smell coming from the kitchen area.

"Uh-oh," he said.

Ricky and I had to dump the coffee and clean the machine. It was a mess of burned milk and gunky melted sugar.

"You don't add the milk and sugar directly to the machine," I told him. "Whoever wants it just adds it to their cup."

"I know that now," said Ricky. "Please don't

tell Diego I messed up! He might not let me be a batboy after all."

"Don't worry," I told him. My own first attempt at coffee had almost been a disaster too. I told him how the coffeepot was spitting steam and rattling like it might explode, and how Wayne put on all his catcher's gear just to turn it off.

"Wish I could have seen that!" said Ricky.

Dylan arrived and saw the rows of bats leaning against the wall.

"What's going on?"

"Never mind. This is Ricky, your temporary replacement."

"Oh, hey!" They shook hands.

"I'm really excited to be a batboy," said Ricky.

"I'm really glad they found a replacement. I don't feel as bad about leaving."

"Where are you going?" Ricky asked him.

"I'm going to be out of town for about a week," said Dylan.

That didn't answer the question. What was he up to?

"Hey, Ricky!" Sammy Solaris was standing in the doorway. "Your brother wants you to translate for him."

"Really? What's going on?"

"A reporter from the *Pine City Press* wants to interview him," said Sammy. "She's going to do a feature on his hitting streak."

"Holy cow! I'll be right there!" Ricky looked at me. "Sorry, I need to go."

"It's cool," I said.

"You're awesome." He slapped my hand and hurried off.

6

icky ran out onto the field halfway through batting practice. Dylan and I were already out there fielding fly balls. Myung Young was out there too, practicing his death-defying catches and showing off for the fans.

"I want to help!" said Ricky.

"Sure thing." I moved over. "Get anything that comes your way."

Ricky pounded his glove a couple of times and watched the batter. Teddy was at the plate, taking his practice swings. He sailed a ball our

way. I took a few steps to my right, thinking I would get it on the first bounce. Ricky charged the ball but misplayed it. It bounced and hit him in the stomach. He fumbled for it, finally got a grip, and threw it toward the bull pen.

"Beat you!" he said.

"It's not a contest," I reminded him.

The next ball went toward Myung Young. He took a step back and waited for it. Ricky ran and leaped. He missed the ball but crashed into Myung. They both sprawled out on the ground.

They were both OK, but Myung was mad. He had a right to be.

"Be more careful," he said. "And stay out of my way."

"Sorry," said Ricky.

Ricky was better after that, just playing the balls that came his way.

"That was fun!" he said as we trotted off the field.

"It's my favorite part of the job," I told him. "And you know, I messed up the first time I did it too. I got in trouble for throwing balls to my friends in the stands."

"Ha. At least I didn't do *that*," he said.

"Hey, Ricky," said Dylan. "I always double-check the bat rack after BP. Come on, I'll show you how." They went into the locker room.

Danny O'Brien was in the dugout. His foot wasn't in a plastic boot anymore, but it was still wrapped up.

"Is your ankle any better?" I asked.

"I'm walking on it, but it'll be a bit longer before I can play baseball. Hey, thanks for loaning me those books! I read them all while the team was on the road. Then I went to the library and checked out some of my own. I returned the ones you lent me. Hope that's OK."

"No problem, and thanks!"

"Which one are you reading now?" asked Wayne Zane.

"N.O.Y.B.," said Danny. "If I tell you, you'll spoil it." He turned the book over so Wayne couldn't see it.

"You're reading *Murder at the Masters*, aren't you?" said Wayne. "I think I saw a golf course on the cover."

"Maybe," said Danny.

"That one's good," said Wayne. He didn't say another word. He just whistled a little song to himself.

"Drat it!" Danny threw the book down.

"What?"

"You were whistling 'Dixie.' I bet the killer is Dixie Douglas, the millionaire heiress who's trying to marry a member of the golf club's senior committee."

Wayne took a breath.

"Ugh! I'm right, aren't I? You've spoiled another ending."

"I didn't even mean to," said Wayne. "Besides, I didn't tell you the part where she's not an heiress at all, she's a con artist."

"You told me just now!"

"I mean, up until I told you, I hadn't told you."

Danny sighed. "I'm still going to finish it." He started reading again.

I had a thought. "Hey, Wayne," I whispered. "Have you read all of the Mike McKay mysteries?"

"I think so," he said. "Why?"

"I want you to spoil one for me."

"Which book?"

"Never Get Back."

"The missing batboy!" He snapped his fingers. "That's probably the best one of all. The ending is amazing."

"Really? What happens?"

"Well, I don't want to spoil it for Danny . . ." He beckoned at me to lean in, and then he whispered, "It ends with a kid finishing a good book."

I groaned.

"Sorry," he said. "I think you should read it, is all."

"Hey, aren't you helping out the Rogues?" Wally asked me.

"Leaving now." I stopped, realizing I'd forgotten something important.

"Good luck," I told Diego. "Can't wait for number twelve."

"Gracias." We slapped hands.

• • •

"Hey, Rogues!" Ernie Hecker's voice carried down from the stands. "Let me know if you need another pitcher!"

"Ugh. He knows where it hurts," said one of the Rogues.

"He's trying to get under our skin. Ignore him," said another player.

"I can come down and throw for a few innings!" Ernie shouted. "Just want to help."

They ignored him.

"So, this new right fielder is supposed to be red-hot at the plate. Diego Pravo," said the first guy. "He's got a hitting streak going. Nine or ten games."

"Eleven," I said. "His name is *Prado*, and he's the *left* fielder."

"OK. But he is red-hot, right?"

"He sure is."

"At least I got that part right."

Ernie kept up his hollering all through the top of the first inning, but he quieted down when Diego came to bat in the bottom of the inning. Diego was leading off for the Porcupines. It used to be Tommy, the third baseman, but Diego was hitting really well and getting on base, so it was good baseball strategy to have him hit first.

The crowd was really excited and started clapping slowly.

"Shh!" Ernie hissed. "He needs to concentrate!"

Diego didn't seem to notice the noise. He got in his stance and waited. The pitcher threw the ball. Diego swung and lined a hit into center field. The crowd went crazy. A big number "12" flashed on the jumbo screen. Pokey the Porcupine mascot jumped up and down for joy.

"Way to go, Diego!" Ernie shouted.

Diego rounded first and headed to second base. The crowd kept cheering.

They started chanting, "Way to go, Di-e-go! Way to go, Di-e-go!"

"I wrote that!" Ernie shouted over the noise.

I worked in the Porcupines' dugout the next day. Ricky helped me with the bat rack and the coffee and didn't make a mess of anything. Maybe he would be a good temporary batboy after all.

As the fans filled the stands, I noticed a few signs that all said the same thing.

WAY TO GO, DIEGO!

The saying had caught on.

"You're becoming a star," I told Diego.

He said something in Spanish, and Ricky said something back.

"He's worried about today," Ricky explained. "He says the number thirteen is unlucky."

"Tell him that's just a superstition."

"I told him it's unlucky for the other team."

"I like the way you think!"

The crowd cheered when Pokey the mascot cruised out onto the field in his golf cart. Spike the junior mascot was with him. Spike was a tough-looking porcupine with spines that looked like a punk rock hairdo. Pokey was at every game, but Spike appeared only on weekends.

"It's Spike!" Ricky pointed. "Diego told me about Spike!" He jumped out onto the field and ran after the golf cart. The two mascots got out and started waving at fans. Ricky waved too. When Spike did cartwheels, Ricky did clumsy

somersaults. When Spike did a little dance, Ricky joined in. He forgot he wasn't dressed up like a porcupine.

Pokey started nudging him back toward the dugout, and Ricky got the message.

"I did tricks with Pokey and Spike!" he said when he got back.

"I saw. You shouldn't have done that, Ricky."

"Sorry, I just got excited." He hung his head.

"It's OK. It's just that *they're* the mascots and *we're* the batboys. We each do our own thing." Then I remembered that Spike once took my place as a batboy for a couple of innings. I told him the story.

"That's funny," he said. "Spike is a good sport."

"Sure is," I said.

A few minutes later, Spike came by the dugout.

"Hi, Abby," I whispered. That was the kid's name who was in the costume. She was a friend from school. Only a few people knew Spike's secret identity.

"Hi, Chad," she said. "Who's the new batboy?"

"Ricky Prado—he's Diego's little brother. He's just going to be here for a few days. I told him not to interfere with your routines anymore."

"Good! He nearly kicked me in the head."

"He was just excited to see you. Did you know you have a fan from Mexico?"

"Really? From Mexico?"

"You're an international star."

The porcupine couldn't turn red, but I had a feeling that Abby was blushing inside the costume.

• • •

Diego led off in the bottom of the first inning. The pitcher threw a couple of balls before Diego took a swing. He hit the ball hard and sent it flying over the outfield fence. The crowd stood and cheered, "Way to go, Di-e-go! Way to go, Di-e-go!" as he circled the bases. They held up their signs. Pokey skipped along, waving at fans, while Spike did cartwheels.

"That's Prado's first home run as a Porcupine!" Victor Snapp announced over the PA system.

I couldn't believe that was his first home run when he had so many hits.

"Hurry—go get your brother's first home run ball," I told Ricky. "Diego will want to keep it."

I hoped it wasn't too late. The ball was just lying out there, waiting for somebody to nab it.

"Sure!" Ricky sped off.

The Porcupines clapped Diego's back and shoulders as he came in, adding, "Thirteen! Thirteen!" to the chant from the crowd.

"*Trece! Trece!*" Luis Quezada said. He was a utility infielder. Grumps put him in a lot as a pinch runner because he was fast.

Diego smiled and sighed in relief.

"Now your home run streak begins!" said Wayne.

"Hey, don't put too much pressure on him," said Sammy.

"Just sayin'," said Wayne.

Diego said something, and this time Luis translated.

"He'll settle for a streak of Porcupine wins."

"Me too," I agreed. But the hitting streak was fun too.

Ricky still wasn't back by the end of the inning. Since the Porcupines weren't batting,

I went to find him. He was in the equipment room, scrubbing a baseball.

"What are you doing?"

"Diego's home run ball was dirty, so I'm trying to scrub it clean. I'm using this super-duper cleaner, but I'm not having much luck." He showed me the ball. He'd practically taken off the logo, and the surface was all scratched up. He was using the wire brush and pink cleanser Wally used in the showers.

"Um, you probably shouldn't use those on leather," I told him.

He gulped. "Really?"

"It might be too much," I said. "Anyway, we'd better get back to the game."

We put the cleanser away and returned to the dugout.

Ricky gave the ball to Diego. He looked at it, baffled.

"*¿Qué es esto?*"

"Your home run ball," said Ricky. His shoulders slumped. "I tried to clean it, but I guess I ruined it."

Diego whispered to his brother in Spanish, and patted him on the head. Ricky whispered back.

"He's a little mad," he confided to me a bit later. "He said it was a nice thought but I should have asked first."

"At least it didn't get chewed up by the world's crankiest cat." I told him how that happened to a ball I tried to get back for Teddy Larrabee, and he started to feel better.

"This ball is in better shape than that one!" he said.

"Yep."

The Porcupines had a great game. They scored ten runs, and the Rogues didn't score any. The crowd chanted, "Way to go, Di-e-go!" until they were hoarse.

In the eighth inning, the Porcupines sent in a relief pitcher. It was Nate Link, who'd taught me his crazy sidewinder pitch. It would take a few minutes for him to warm up.

I went into the locker room to get a shoe brush for Myung to brush the mud off his spikes. Danny was there, his leg stretched out on the bench. I hadn't realized he'd slipped out of the dugout.

"How's it going?" I asked.

"I'm good," he said. "Just needed to rest this sore ankle."

"You're missing a good game."

"I know."

I got the brush from the equipment box. Danny stopped me on the way out.

"Hey, Chad," he said. "Did you ever hear of Wally Pipp?"

I thought hard. "I don't think so."

"He was a first baseman for the Yankees. One day he had a headache, and he sat out the game. The manager put in a guy named Lou Gehrig to play for him."

"I've heard of *him*," I said.

"Of course you have. Lou Gehrig played the next twenty-one hundred and twenty-nine games. He didn't miss a single one until he got really sick. So Wally Pipp was . . . well, he got 'Wally Pipped.' That's what they call it now, when you sit out a couple of games and end up losing your job."

I remembered what Casey had said. Grumps would probably make Diego the permanent left fielder.

"I hope that doesn't happen to you," I said.

"Me, neither. That's why I want to talk to you. Do you have a card for a guy who's the opposite of Wally Pipp?"

"I don't have a card for Lou Gehrig."

"It doesn't have to be Lou Gehrig," he said. "Just some guy who came back from an injury and was better than ever. Like Tommy John, only an outfielder."

"I don't know," I said. I would have to talk to my uncle Rick. He knew everything there was about baseball, and he would know just the right player. "I'll see what I can do."

"Thanks, buddy."

There were twice as many signs waving in the ballpark on Sunday. I was working in the visitors' dugout. Ernie Hecker shouted his usual comments at the Rogues, but when the Porcupines came up to bat, he started the crowd chanting again, "Way to go, Di-e-go! Way to go, Di-e-go!"

They stopped when Diego came to the plate. He struck out in his first at-bat.

"Nice try!" Ernie shouted. "You'll get it next time!" I think he meant it!

The crowd chanted again in the third

inning when Diego came up again. This time he drew a walk. The crowd clapped, but it was disappointed. He'd reached first base, but it wasn't a hit. Walks didn't count for a hitting streak.

"Pitch to him this time!" Ernie shouted in the sixth inning when Diego came to the plate for the third time. The pitcher did, but Diego struck out again.

The crowd groaned.

When Diego came up in the eighth inning, the crowd was too nervous to chant. It was probably his last at-bat of the game, and his last chance to keep the hitting streak going. I glanced up and saw a lot of people covering their eyes. They couldn't watch. Others had their caps turned upside down, rally cap style, and they all had their fingers crossed.

"Come on," I muttered. "You can do it."

The pitcher got two strikes. Diego didn't swing on the next pitch, and it was ruled a ball. He swung at the fourth pitch and knocked it foul. Every pitch made my heart skip.

On the fifth pitch, he hit a ground ball just past the third baseman and scampered to first base. He was definitely safe, but the play might be ruled an error. If the official scorer decided that it was an error, then Diego's hitting streak would be dead. Errors didn't count for a hitting streak.

The scorer's decision finally flashed up on the board. "HIT"! The word flashed three times and was replaced with a big "14." The crowd clapped like mad and shouted, "Way to go, Di-e-go!" until he tipped his hat and took a little bow.

• • •

The Rogues' three-game series against the Porcupines was done. I had to spend extra time helping the Rogues pack up and load their bus. The Pines' locker room was mostly cleared out when I got there, but Diego was still there. So was Ricky.

"Great game," I said.

"Gracias," said Diego. He didn't look at all happy.

"What's wrong?"

Diego spoke in Spanish. Ricky translated.

"He's scared the streak will end."

I didn't know what to say. The streak *would* end. It had to. It would be fun while it lasted, but it couldn't last forever.

Diego spoke again.

"He's heard you have magic cards," said Ricky. "Can he please have one, to keep his streak going?"

"Sure, but I don't know which card will help him."

Diego said something in Spanish. I made out the English words: "Joltin' Joe."

"There's a player named Joltin' Joe?" Ricky asked.

"It must be a nickname," I said.

Wally, the clubhouse manager, walked by with a bag of equipment. "Wally, was there ever a player called 'Joltin' Joe'?" I asked.

"There sure was. That's what they called Joe DiMaggio." Wally set the bag down and took a deep breath. "In 1941, he went fifty-six straight games with a hit in each game. It's the longest hitting streak in the big leagues. That record's never been beat. Nobody's even come close."

"Do you remember it?" Ricky asked him.

Wally laughed. "I'm old, but not that old."

"I don't have a card for Joe DiMaggio." My oldest cards were from the mid-1950s, when Grandpa started buying them. "Who else had a long hitting streak?" I asked Wally.

"Pete Rose had a good one," he said. "So did Paul Molitor."

"I probably have a card for one of them," I said. "Maybe even both."

Diego spoke quickly. He seemed excited.

"He says, 'Thank you, Kid Magic,'" said Ricky.

"No problemo," I said. I wasn't sure if that was really Spanish or not, but Diego understood.

Dylan came out of the equipment room. I was glad he was still there. It was my last chance to talk to him before he left.

"Excited for your trip?" I asked.

"Sure."

Of course, he still didn't tell me where he was going.

I changed into my street clothes and we headed out together.

"I'm worried about leaving," he admitted once we were outside.

"You are?"

"Ricky is a nice kid and a hard worker, but have you noticed that he . . ." Dylan paused. He didn't like to say anything bad about anyone. "He tries a little too hard," he said.

"What happened today?"

"It involved the laundry machine. And bleach. And baseball gloves."

"Oh, no."

"It was a disaster," he said. "Maybe I should cancel my trip. Ricky's just not ready to sub for me."

"No way," I said. "You've been looking forward to it."

"I really have," he admitted. "You'll have to work in the visiting dugout so Wally can keep an eye on Ricky."

"You're probably right." I would miss working with the Pines during the game.

"Oh, by the way," said Dylan, "Danny said to remind you. He didn't say what. He just said to remind you. And that you would know."

"I do know. Thanks." He wanted to remind me to get him a baseball card that was the opposite of Wally Pipp.

"Have a great week," said Dylan.

"You too!" We slapped hands, and I hurried home.

I wanted to talk to Uncle Rick. I would ask him what card might help Danny heal so he could play again. I could ask him about the best card for Diego too. I slowed a few steps, realizing I was in a pickle.

I couldn't help both Diego and Danny! If Diego's hitting streak kept going, Danny wouldn't get his starting job back. No baseball card had enough magic in it to help the Porcupines have two full-time left fielders. And even if one of them moved somewhere else in the outfield, it would mean something happened to Myung or Brian.

There was no way out of it. Somebody had to lose.

I talked to Uncle Rick over video-chat. He was in Colorado. He held his laptop up to the window of his hotel room so I could see the mountains. He travels a lot for his job.

"That's a great view!" I told him.

"I wish I had time to see the ballpark here in Denver," he said. "But I have to be in Tennessee tomorrow." I was surprised there was a major league ballpark he hadn't seen. "So how are your Porcupines doing? I read on a baseball blog you have the hottest hitter in Single-A."

"We do!" I told him about Diego's hitting streak and worked my way around to telling him about the pickle I was in. I'd promised I would help both Diego and Danny, but I couldn't put one card against another, and I couldn't pick sides.

"Sometimes baseball is a hard game," Uncle Rick agreed.

"What should I do?"

"Maybe you need to bench yourself," he said. "You're a batboy. You don't have to take care of the players; just take care of the bats."

"OK," I said. He was probably right, but it didn't feel right.

• • •

Dad popped into my room that evening. "We got a reminder call from the library," he said. "You have a book due tomorrow."

"Oh, right." The two weeks had flown by.

I had to *find* the book before I could finish reading it, and I wanted to finish reading it before I returned it.

"Can you renew it on the computer? We still have seven more home games, so it'll be a while before I can get to the library."

"Sure," he said. "But if it's the missing book, you'll have to pay for it eventually."

"I know. Next time I have a day off, I'll search the house top to bottom."

"I'll renew it," he said. "But don't forget you need to find it."

"I won't." I'd forgotten about the book. I looked all over my room, but it was useless. The book had disappeared, just like Charlie himself.

• • •

When I walked into the locker room on Monday, Ricky had a big grin on his face.

"Guess what I did?" he asked.

"What?"

"You'll see!"

Uh-oh. When Ricky did things on his own, they tended to end badly.

I opened my locker and saw what he was talking about. He'd cleaned my locker. He had not thrown anything away, or hosed anything down, or applied a fresh coat of paint. He'd just cleaned it, and he'd done a great job.

"Hey, thanks. You didn't have to do that."

He smiled. *"¡No problema!"*

"Is your brother already out taking batting practice?"

"Yeah. He's been starting earlier and earlier. All he wants to do is practice. He thinks the second the hitting streak ends, the fans won't like him anymore and he'll be back on the bench."

"I think the fans will still like him, whatever happens." Besides, Diego was a rising star. Everybody said so.

I found the coffee machine gurgling away and the bat rack set up. Both were done perfectly. When we went out for BP, Ricky fielded his own territory and didn't get in anyone's way. When Pokey came out on the field, Ricky didn't run over and try to be a part of the act. When Sammy sent Ricky to the snack bar to get his traditional pre-game corn dog, he was back in a flash.

"I think he's going to work out," Wally whispered to me before I headed over to the other dugout.

"Me too."

We were playing the Farmington Weevils. The Pines scored some runs, but Diego didn't get his first hit until his third time at the plate. He scorched the ball past the shortstop and into the outfield.

After the game, Pokey drove his golf cart across the outfield, flying a flag with the number "15" on it. The crowd went crazy. It seemed like they were more excited for the hit than the fact that the Porcupines won the game.

When I got back to the Pines' locker room, I found a note taped to my locker.

THANKS, MAN. I REALLY APPRECIATE IT. SORRY I COULDN'T STICK AROUND AND SAY SO IN PERSON. DON'T WORRY. I'LL DROP IT OFF BEFORE I GO.

—D.

It must have been from Danny, since Dylan was away and Diego wouldn't have written a note in English. But I didn't know what he was thanking me for. I also didn't know what he was dropping off or where he was going or when. It was another mystery for Mike McKay to solve.

• • •

Part of the mystery was solved the next day. I saw that Danny O'Brien's locker had been cleaned out. I felt like I'd been kicked in the stomach.

"What happened?" Was Danny cut loose because of his injury?

"He's been traded," said Brian Daniels. "Multi-way deal that gets pitching to the Rogues and a hot rookie infielder for us. It also sends Danny to the Cougars."

"Wow." I remembered the last series against

the Cougars. Their left fielder wasn't very good. Danny would be a big improvement, once he got healthy. "I'm going to miss him."

"Me too," said Brian. "He was like a brother to me."

"A twin brother," said Wayne. Danny and Brian looked a lot alike, and it was easy to get them confused.

"Practically," Brian agreed. "But it's a good move for him. We have a lot of good outfielders at Double-A and Triple-A. It's hard to move up. Over there, Danny will have a better chance to get promoted."

I had to sit down. I was feeling a bit dazed. I knew that players got shuffled around in baseball, but I'd worked with mostly the same group of players since I'd become a batboy.

"Hey, it's all good news," said Wayne.

"Good news for Danny. Good news for the Pines. Good news for Diego."

"I know."

But how come it didn't feel like good news?

few days later, on the last day of the home stand, Diego hit safely in his twenty-first consecutive game. It was a new record for the Prairie League. The crowd chanted, "Way to go, Di-e-go!" until long after the last out. Diego came out and waved his cap at the crowd.

It had been a great series of games for the Porcupines. They'd swept the Rogues, won three of four against the Weevils, and taken two out of three against the West Valley Varmints. They'd gained a lot of ground in the league standings and seemed bound for the playoffs.

I helped the Varmints load up their bus and then went to the Porcupines' locker room.

Diego was cleaning out his locker. Several of the Porcupines were gathered around, watching in silence.

"What's going on?" I asked.

Ricky answered. "Diego has been called up. All the way to Triple-A!"

"Congratulations!" That was great for him. It was what every player dreamed of. Diego would be just one step away from the major leagues. But I felt another kick to my stomach. Diego had become one of my favorite players.

"I can't wait to see you on TV in the big leagues," I told him.

Ricky started to translate, but Diego nodded. He understood. *"Gracias,"* he said. He said a lot more, and Ricky tried to keep up.

"He says he will see you all when you get called up, and he will miss you until then, and he hopes every team is as nice as you guys, and he will miss Wayne's jokes."

"He'll miss Wayne's jokes?" asked Sammy. "Are you sure you know Spanish?"

"Pretty sure," said Ricky, his face puzzled.

Diego spoke again, and Ricky nodded.

"He couldn't have done it without you," Ricky said to me.

"Me?" I said.

"He didn't believe in the magic before, but now he does. He says thank you."

Diego reached into his pocket and passed me a tattered baseball card.

Ozzie Virgil.

I had forgotten all about that card.

"But this was in . . . ," I started to say.

"The library book that I gave to Danny,"

said Ricky. "I found it in your locker when I was cleaning it out. It was with a sticky note that said 'Remember to give to Danny,' so I gave it to him."

My head spun. I must have brought the book to work with the others without realizing it, left it in my locker, and not noticed it in the mess. The sticky note was left over from the other three books I *did* give to Danny.

No wonder I couldn't find it at home!

"How did Diego get the baseball card? I was using it as a bookmark."

"Danny gave it to him before he left. He said it was Diego's turn."

"Oh." But how had the card helped either one of them? Ozzie Virgil didn't have a miraculous comeback after an injury, and he didn't have a long hitting streak. He was just a guy who played baseball for a while.

"Thank you, and good-bye for now," said Diego slowly.

He shook my hand and then went through the group, shaking everybody's hands.

Wayne was last. "Way to go, Diego," he said.

"Hey, and thanks for teaching me how to be a batboy," Ricky told me. "It was the most fun I've ever had."

"Adios, amigo," I told him.

"No," he said. *"Hasta luego. Adios* means 'Good-bye.' *Hasta luego* is 'See you later.'"

• • •

I got on video-chat with Uncle Rick that night so I could tell him what happened.

"The same card worked for both players?" he said. "That's funny."

"They both got what they wanted, sort of," I said. "But Ozzie Virgil never did anything special. That's the part I don't get."

He frowned. "'Nothing special'? Are you kidding me?"

"His stats were really average," I protested. "He kept getting sent back to the minor leagues and then coming back up."

"He stayed in the game, Chad," said Uncle Rick. "He was up and down his whole career, but he hung in there. And he's not in the Hall of Fame, but he made his little mark on baseball history. He paved the way for other great players from the Dominican Republic. Everybody from Felipe Alou to David Ortiz."

"Sure, but . . ."

"I've always been a big fan of guys like Ozzie Virgil," said Uncle Rick. "I think they *are* special. There aren't enough superstars to staff all thirty teams. We need the guys who hang in there."

"I know." The Porcupines didn't have any

big stars, at least not now that Diego was gone, but what would they be without Wayne or Sammy?

"Maybe Ozzie Virgil helped those guys see the big picture," said Uncle Rick. "Every career is going to have some high points and some setbacks."

"Hmm . . . that makes a lot of sense," I said.

I was going to have to think the same way about being a batboy. The team had lost two good guys, but we'd won a bunch of games and were headed for the playoffs for the second year in a row. I would have to hang in there and not feel sorry for myself, especially when Diego and Danny were both chasing their dreams.

ylan called me the next day. He was
back from his trip.

"Want to hang out?" he asked.

"Sure. Want to bike to the library?"

He took a while to answer. "Sure," he said
finally, but he didn't sound like he really wanted
to go.

I realized why when we were out on our
ride. Dylan had to stop every few minutes and
take a break.

"Sorry to hold you up," he said.

"What's wrong?"

"I'll explain, but you have to promise not to tease me."

"I would never do that," I said. "Well . . . unless it's something really silly."

He laughed. "It's not that bad. I was at horse camp last week. My butt is still sore!"

"Hey, that sounds great! Why would I tease you about going to horse camp?"

"Well, here's the thing. There's only one close by, and it's called the West Valley Riding School for Girls. Lately they've allowed boys to go, but they haven't changed the name."

"Glad you could go. Why should girls have all the fun?"

"Thanks, Chad."

"¡No problema!"

He cycled on, sore butt and all, and we made it to the library. Dylan checked out two books about alpacas.

"You've moved on?"

"They had some at the horse camp," he explained. "I liked them."

"You can't ride an alpaca."

"I think that's what I like best about them!"

I checked out *Never Get Back* for the second time, and this time I read it all the way through without misplacing the book. It was a great mystery. The ending really surprised me. But I won't say what happened. I don't want to spoil it for you.

About the Author

Kurtis Scaletta's previous books include *Mudville*, which *Booklist* called "a gift from the baseball gods" and named one of their 2009 Top 10 Sports Books for Youth. Kurtis lives in Minneapolis with his wife and son and some cats. He roots for the Minnesota Twins and the Saint Paul Saints. Find out more about him at www.kurtisscaletta.com.

About the Artist

Ethen Beavers has illustrated a bunch of comics and children's books, including the bestselling NERDS series by Michael Buckley. He lives in California and likes fishing and his wife. He roots for the San Francisco Giants and loves to watch *The Natural*. You can see more of his drawings online at http://cretineb.deviantart.com.

Come on into the **Reading Topps® Clubhouse!**

Check out these other winning titles in the Topps League Story series featuring Chad, Dylan, Spike, and the Pine City Porcupines.

Keep an eye out for another
Topps League Story, Book Five: You're Out!